Tyler the Fish
and Marty the Sturgeon

by Meaghan Fisher
art by Sandra Burns

Gypsy
Publications

Published in 2015, by Gypsy Publications
Troy, OH 45373, U.S.A.
www.GypsyPublications.com

Fisher, Meaghan
Tyler the Fish and Marty the Sturgeon
Story by Meaghan Fisher; Illustrated by Sandra Burns

ISBN 978-1-938768-63-7 (paperback)

Library of Congress Control Number
2015950585

Edited by Jon Williams
Book Design by Tim Rowe

To Lake Erie and all the wonderful creatures that live there. May you always stay beautiful and safe.

There once was a little bass named Tyler. He lived in one of the Great Lakes in Ohio called Lake Erie. Tyler had many friends and he often would play with them in the lake waters until his mother would call him home for supper.

One day, Tyler and his friend Jimmy were playing Fish Tag in the lake waters when they noticed the fish near them were suddenly swimming away. "Help!" they all cried as they hurried away.

"Why is everyone swimming away so fast?" Tyler asked Jimmy.

Suddenly, the lake grew darker.
"Tyler," said Jimmy, "why is it so dark?"

Tyler was about to answer his friend when a large wave came abruptly from behind them, causing them to turn around. As they both turned they saw a large, scary-looking fish hovering in front of them.

"Hello, you two!" said the scary large fish.

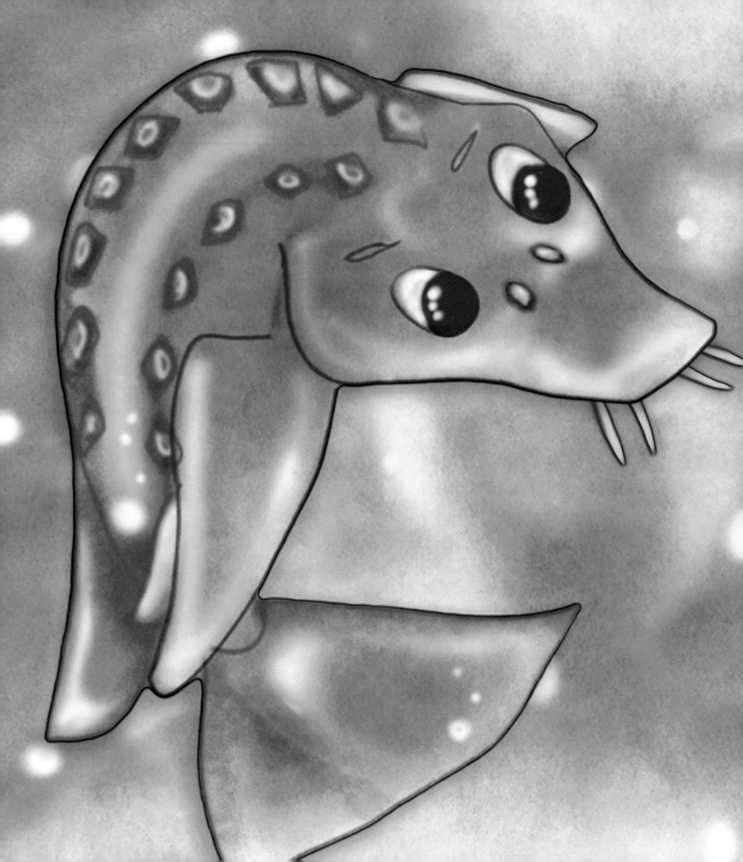

Tyler and Jimmy screamed in fear and began
to swim away as fast as they could, but with one
fast swoop of the large fish's fin, he managed to
scoop them back.

"Wait! Don't be afraid, little fish," he said. "My
name is Marty and I don't mean any harm. I am a
sturgeon, a fish that is near extinction, and I need
your help. I ran into a fisherman's hook and I just
wanted to see if you two could take it out of my fin."

"Oh, my," cried Jimmy and Tyler, "that must hurt!"

"Yes, it does and I was really hoping to find some kind fish to help me pull it out!"

"Don't worry!" said Tyler. "With our help, you will have that hook out of your fin in no time."

Tyler and Jimmy both swam up to the top of Marty's fin.
"Okay," shouted Tyler. "One, two, three, PULL!"
Both little fish pulled on the hook as hard as they could.
Soon, the hook gave way.

"Oh...thank you, little fish!" cried Marty with excitement. "How can I ever thank you?"

"By not eating us," replied Jimmy in fear.

"Oh, you!" exclaimed Marty as he grabbed Tyler and Jimmy and hugged them tight. "I would never do anything like that. You two helped me. Besides, I eat worms, I wouldn't eat you two!"

"Hey," said Tyler, "can you tell us what 'extinction' means?"

"Yes, I can," replied Marty. "Extinction means that a species will be all gone, if people are not careful. In my case, I am a sturgeon, which is a type of fish, and I live here in Lake Erie, like you. I am afraid there are not many sturgeons like myself left anymore. So it's important for fisherman not to fish for us."

"I have an idea," said Tyler. "How would you like to come to my house for dinner and talk to my family about your species? We have never met a fish near extinction before!"

"Okay, then," said Marty. "I would love to meet your folks!"

Marty went with them back to Tyler's house, where he met Tyler's parents. Soon they all gathered around the dinner table to eat.

Jimmy, Tyler, and his parents had a great time at dinner, listening to Marty talk about endangered fish and animals.

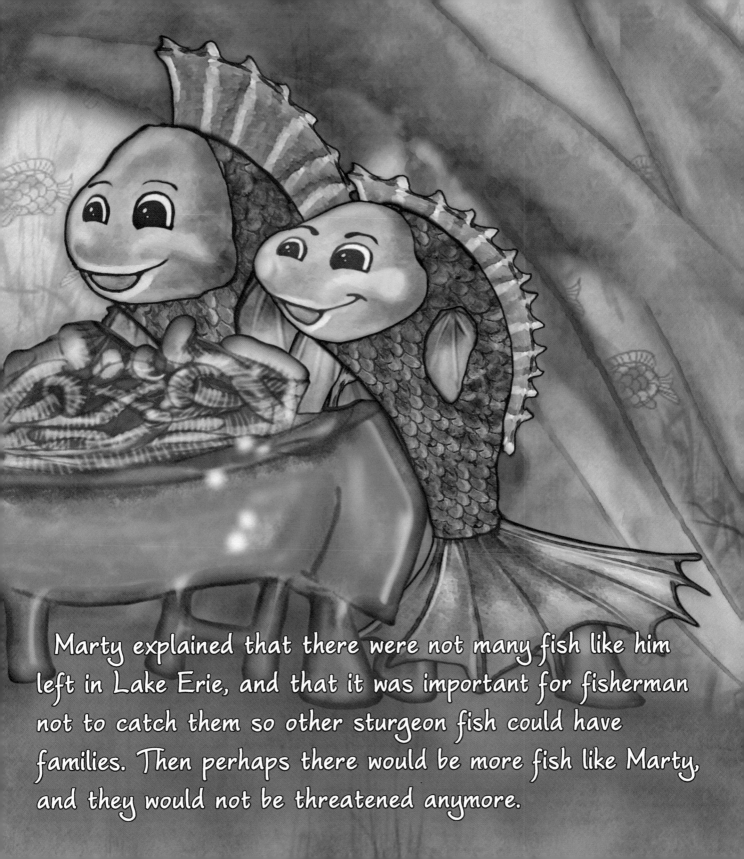

Marty explained that there were not many fish like him left in Lake Erie, and that it was important for fisherman not to catch them so other sturgeon fish could have families. Then perhaps there would be more fish like Marty, and they would not be threatened anymore.

Later that night, when Tyler was tucked into his fishy bed, he lay awake thinking about Marty, sturgeons, and extinction. Tyler realized how important Marty was to Lake Erie because his species was near extinction.

He also realized that he had been afraid when he first met Marty. Even though it was sometimes scary to meet new fish, he wouldn't be afraid anymore because that fish could end up being a good friend.

CPSIA information can be obtained at www.ICGtesting.com
Printed in the USA
BVIW12n1734100818
524092BV00007B/25